DreamWorks DRAGONS

How to Start a DRAGON ACADEMY

adapted by Erica David

Ready-to-Read

Simon Spotlight

New York   London   Toronto   Sydney   New Delhi

Vikings and dragons
used to be enemies.
Then Hiccup met his dragon, Toothless.
They became best friends.

Now Vikings and dragons
live side by side on Berk.

Most Vikings are happy to share
their home with dragons.
But sometimes the dragons
get into trouble.

The dragons scare fish
out of the Vikings' nets.
They chase sheep out of their pens.
And they steal food.

Usually the Vikings
can forgive the dragons.
But some Vikings are angry
when the dragons eat their food.
They are trying to store food
for the winter freeze that is coming.

There is one Viking named Mildew
who is very upset.
The dragons ate his entire field of
cabbage!

"Stoick, you need to put those dragons in cages!" Mildew shouts. "If you don't, they will eat us out of house and home!"

"They don't mean any harm,"
Hiccup replies.
"They are just dragons being dragons."
Chief Stoick tells Mildew
he will handle the dragons.

That night Hiccup asks Stoick if he
can help with the dragons.
"You?" Stoick asks.
"If anyone can control them,
I can," Hiccup says.
Stoick decides to give Hiccup a chance.

The next day Hiccup and Toothless
go to the village square.
Hiccup feels confident that he can
get the dragons under control.

The dragons are up to
their usual tricks.
Hiccup watches as a Deadly Nadder
sneaks up to a house to
steal a loaf of bread.

Hiccup chases after the Nadder
and places a hand on his nose.
"No!" Hiccup says firmly.

The Deadly Nadder listens
and drops the bread.

But while Hiccup is training
one dragon, other dragons
make trouble all over the village.
Hiccup tries to stop them
but it is no use.
It begins to look like he is helping
the dragons break things!

Hiccup realizes he cannot
train the dragons alone.

The next day Hiccup invites his
friends and their dragons to the arena.
"The dragons are out of control,"
he says. "We want them
to live in our world
without destroying it, but
they can't without our help."

Hiccup shows his friends
how to scratch under a dragon's
chin to get it to drop stolen food.

It seems like they are making progress.
But when they head into the village
to find dragons to train,
there are no dragons in sight.

Suddenly there is a loud noise!
Hiccup and his friends rush
toward the noise.
When they arrive, they are shocked.

The dragons broke into
the village storehouse.
They ate all the food
that the Vikings were storing
for the freeze!

Even Toothless is guilty.

Soon Mildew and the other Vikings arrive.

They are very angry.

"You need to send these dragons away!" Mildew shouts.

"You're right, Mildew,"
Chief Stoick says.
"We will cage them tonight, and
Hiccup will send them away
in the morning."

At dinner Hiccup and his friends
are very sad.
They don't want to send their
dragons away.
But Hiccup has an idea.

"The dragons are going to do
what they're going to do,"
Hiccup tells his friends.
"It's in their nature.
We just have to learn to use it."

The next day Hiccup and
his friends decide to work with
the dragons—not against them.

The dragons scare fish
into the Vikings' nets and
chase sheep into their pens.

The dragons plant food
instead of stealing it.
They even help Mildew
plant his field!

"Great job, dragons!"
the Vikings cheer.
Chief Stoick is so proud of Hiccup
and his friends, he gives them
their very own dragon training
academy.

Hiccup is excited.
He can't wait to begin.
"Dragons are powerful, amazing
creatures," he says.
"And I'm going to learn everything
about them."

DREAMWORKS
DRAGONS
How to
PICK YOUR
DRAGON

adapted by Erica David

Ready-to-Read

Simon Spotlight

New York   London   Toronto   Sydney   New Delhi

Chief Stoick was a proud leader.
He did everything the Viking way.
But sometimes the Viking way
was the hard way.

His son, Hiccup, knew another way.
It was the dragon way.
Dragons could help make life easier.
Hiccup convinced Stoick to learn
how to fly a dragon.

Hiccup and his dragon, Toothless, offered to teach Stoick to ride. Stoick was eager to learn. "Whoa, Dad," Hiccup said. "Before you ride, you have to show the dragon he can trust you."

Hiccup placed Stoick's hand
on Toothless' snout.
Toothless closed his eyes
and lowered his head.
It was a sign of trust.

Stoick was eager for
the next lesson.
He jumped onto Toothless' back
and took off into the sky.

Hiccup warned Stoick to go slowly.
But he didn't listen.
Hiccup frowned.
His dad had a lot to learn.

The next morning,
Hiccup couldn't find Toothless.
He looked all over for him.
At last, Stoick appeared.
Stoick was riding Toothless.

Stoick was excited.
"We've been all over the village,"
Stoick said. "With Toothless,
being chief has never been so easy!"

"But, Dad," Hiccup said,
"Toothless is my dragon.
You can't just take him."
Stoick looked thoughtful.
"All right, so find me a dragon
of my own," Stoick replied.

Hiccup took Stoick to the
Dragon Training Academy.
Hiccup's friends were eager
to help the chief pick a dragon.

Snotlout brought out Hookfang.
"He is a Monstrous Nightmare,
the only dragon strong enough for
big men like us," he told the chief.

Next, Astrid showed off
her dragon, Stormfly.
"Just because she is beautiful,
it doesn't mean she's not tough,"
Astrid said.

Finally, Fishlegs introduced
his dragon, Meatlug.
"How could you not love
a Gronckle?" he asked Stoick.

Stoick liked all the dragons.
But he couldn't find one he liked
as much as Toothless.

Suddenly, a message arrived
for Chief Stoick.
It said that one of his fishing boats
was in trouble!
Stoick and Hiccup hopped onto
Toothless' back and flew
to the rescue!

The fishing boat was under attack
by a Thunderdrum dragon.

He was stealing the Vikings' fish!

Stoick fought the Thunderdrum
and captured him.
He was very impressed by
the dragon's strength.
"This is the one, Hiccup!
I've found my dragon!" Stoick said.

Stoick brought the Thunderdrum back
to the Dragon Training Academy.
Then he asked Hiccup
to help train his new dragon.

"Be gentle, Dad. Remember,
he has to trust you," Hiccup said.
But Stoick didn't listen.
He and the Thunderdrum
fought and fought . . .

. . . until the Thunderdrum escaped!
Stoick and Hiccup tracked
the dragon to a cave far away.
Another dragon was there, too.

There, they discovered that the Thunderdrum had a secret. The dragon's friend was hurt! "He's trying to help his friend!" Stoick said. "That's why he took our fish!"

Stoick sent Hiccup to get help
for the wounded dragon.
As soon as Hiccup left, a pack of
wild boars charged the cave!
It was up to Stoick and the
Thunderdrum to fight them.

Stoick gently placed his hand on the Thunderdrum's snout. "I want to help. Trust me," he told the dragon.

The Thunderdrum closed his eyes
and lowered his head.
Again, it was a sign of trust.

Stoick took off the dragon's muzzle, then climbed onto its back.

They fought the wild boars
as a team! And they won!

Later, Hiccup returned with
help for the wounded dragon.
By that time, Stoick and the
Thunderdrum were old friends.
"Look at us, we're bonded,"
Stoick said.

Hiccup smiled.
His dad had just learned
an important lesson.

The Viking way could also be
the dragon way.

DREAMWORKS

DRAGONS

How to
DEFEND YOUR
DRAGON

adapted by Ellie O'Ryan

Ready-to-Read

Simon Spotlight

New York   London   Toronto   Sydney   New Delhi

In this story, while Hiccup is trying to help Toothless, he stays outside during a lightning storm. This is very dangerous, and in real life you should never be outside when you see lightning, even if it seems far away. If you see lightning when you are outside, you should find shelter immediately. Remember, you don't have a dragon to protect you—stay safe!

Living with dragons can be great—
but it is not always easy.
Some are so big that when they land
on the roof, the house falls down!

Hiccup knows what to do.
First he draws some plans.
Then the Vikings build metal perches
for the dragons.

Will Hiccup's idea work?
Stormfly soars toward the perch.
Then she lands on it!
"Yes!" cheers Hiccup.

Dark clouds race across the sky.
A storm is brewing—a big storm.
Thunder booms. Lightning strikes.
"Whoa," Hiccup says. "The lightning
is hitting everywhere!"
The Vikings are worried.
They think when lightning strikes
that the god Thor is angry.

Stoick and Gobber remember the
last time lightning hit the village.
They thought Thor was punishing
a thief. When the Vikings sent the
thief away, the lightning stopped.

But why is Thor mad now?
Maybe if the Vikings can learn
the answer, they can keep the
village safe.

Crack! Boom!
More lightning strikes.
One bolt almost hits Toothless!

Many houses are burning.
The Vikings and the dragons work
together to put out the fires.
At last the storm ends.
But fixing the damage has just
begun.

Mildew points at Toothless.
"Thor is angry with us because of the Night Fury," he shouts.

Mildew tells everyone that they must send Toothless away.

He says that is the only way to keep the village safe.

Hiccup knows that Mildew is wrong.
He has got to come up with another
plan. But what?

"If I were Thor, I would want
a giant statue," Snotlout says.
Hiccup thinks that is a great idea!
Everyone works hard to build
a huge statue of Thor.
The metal statue shines in the sun.
"I really think Thor is going to like
this!" says Hiccup.

Everyone is impressed—except Mildew. He still wants to send Toothless away.
"You are fools, all of you!" Mildew yells.

Suddenly, the sky grows dark.
A new storm is coming.
It is even bigger than the last one!
More lightning strikes the houses
and the perches. Some bolts even hit
the new statue of Thor.

Tuffnut and Ruffnut love
watching the storm wreck things.
"Nobody blows stuff up like Thor!"
Tuffnut says.

Everyone can see that the statue
did not work.
Mildew convinces the others
to get rid of Toothless.
They march to Hiccup's house.

"Get Toothless to a safe place,"
Stoick tells Hiccup.
Hiccup does not want Toothless
to go away.
But he is determined to protect
his friend.

When Stoick opens the door,
Mildew says, "Give up the dragon!"
"You are too late," says Stoick.
"He is gone."

Mildew refuses to give up.
"Find the Night Fury!" he orders.

Meanwhile, Hiccup and Toothless
fly into the clouds.
A new storm is brewing—
and it's a big one.

Toothless tries to dodge the
lightning, but one bolt strikes his
metal tail fin.
The dragon spins out of control!

Hiccup and Toothless crash
in the forest.
"You okay, bud?" Hiccup asks.
Toothless will be fine, but the metal
on his tail fin is still glowing.

"That is where the lightning hit," Hiccup realizes. He remembers how lightning struck the metal statue and the metal perches, too.

Just then Mildew and the villagers
find them. They capture Toothless
and take him to the dock.

They want to send Toothless away
forever!
This is Hiccup's last chance
to save his friend.

Hiccup points up at the sky. "The lightning is hitting the metal," Hiccup explains.

Then the lightning hits more metal,
and Hiccup is knocked down
by the force of the lightning strike.
He falls in the water!

Toothless breaks free and dives
into the ocean. He grabs Hiccup
and swims for the surface as fast
as he can.
When Hiccup finally wakes up,
he does not remember anything.

Stoick explains how Hiccup proved
that the lightning was only hitting
metal objects.
Thor was not angry at Toothless.
Now Toothless does not have to leave!

Now everyone in Berk
knows what Hiccup has known
all along.
There is no better friend
in the world than Toothless!

DREAMWORKS

DRAGONS

How to
RAISE THREE
DRAGONS

adapted by Ellie O'Ryan

Ready-to-Read

Simon Spotlight

New York   London   Toronto   Sydney   New Delhi

Hiccup's new invention,
the Thunder-Ear,
was finally ready.
He couldn't wait to test it!

Stoick had never seen anything
like the Thunder-Ear.
"It can track dragon sounds
from miles away," Hiccup explained.

Stoick leaned close to the
Thunder-Ear.
He heard Fishlegs and Meatlug
singing.
But they were very far away.
The Thunder-Ear worked!

Then Stoick heard something
even worse.
"Tell them to stop singing,"
he said.
But the terrible noise wasn't
Fishlegs and Meatlug.
It was three baby
Thunderdrum dragons!

Stoick's dragon, Thornado,
was a Thunderdrum, too.
He recognized their cries
and zoomed off to find them.
They were all by themselves
on a sea stack.

Hiccup didn't want to leave
the baby Thunderdrums alone.
But Stoick said they were too loud
to live in the village.
"They'll be okay on their own," he
told Hiccup.
"Thunderdrums are the toughest
dragons in the world!"

At dawn the next morning Hiccup
jumped out of bed.
What was that terrible noise?
It was the Thunderdrum dragons!
They had followed Hiccup and Stoick
back to Berk.
And they were out of control!

The baby dragons
zoomed through houses,
crashed into food carts,
and even scared the sheep!

"Can you help me wrangle them into the Academy?" Hiccup shouted. "I thought you'd never ask!" Astrid replied.

"Get those troublemakers off the island now!" Stoick ordered, once Thornado had calmed the three baby Thunderdrums. "Don't you think we should train them?" Hiccup asked.

Stoick thought about it.
Thornado was a Thunderdrum,
and he was a great dragon.
Maybe the baby Thunderdrums
would be useful, too,
but only if Hiccup could train them.

"I guess the first thing we should do is name them!" Hiccup yelled.
The Thunderdrums were so loud that they drowned out everyone else!

The friends decided to call them
Bing, Bam, and Boom.
Noisy names for noisy dragons!

"Let's try some training,"
Hiccup said.
At first Bing, Bam, and Boom
did what Hiccup wanted.
But then the trouble started.

Bing, Bam, and Boom roared so loudly
that Hiccup flew across the arena.
When Astrid told them to stay,
they flew in circles.
Snotlout set up some targets,
but they knocked him down instead!
They even swiped Fishlegs' sword!

At last the Thunderdrums were calm.
"We're finally getting through
to them," said Hiccup.
But he was wrong.
It wasn't the training that
made the Thunderdrums behave.
It was Thornado!

Bing, Bam, and Boom were
perfectly behaved with Thornado.
They wanted to be just like him.
And when Thornado flew out of the
arena, the babies followed him!
"Close the gates!" yelled Hiccup.
But it was too late!

Once more Bing, Bam, and Boom
raced through the village.
They shrieked, roared,
and wrecked everything!

"The Thunderdrums have to go,"
Stoick ordered.

Everyone worked together to bring
Bing, Bam, and Boom
to a new home on Dragon Island.
"Here you can be as loud as you want,"
Hiccup told them.
"It will be great!"

Then Hiccup, Toothless, and the others flew away from Dragon Island. Far below, the baby Thunderdrums looked as sad as Hiccup felt.

Back at the village Hiccup found
a big surprise.
Bing, Bam, and Boom had
followed him home again.

Stoick was not happy to see Bing, Bam, and Boom.
"It looks like Thornado and I need to give you a hand," he told Hiccup.

Thornado led the baby Thunderdrums
back to Dragon Island.
Hiccup and Fishlegs followed
on their dragons.

Hiccup said good-bye
to Bing, Bam, and Boom again.
They started to cry.
That made Hiccup feel even worse.

"Don't look back, son," Stoick said
as they flew away.
But when Hiccup heard a scary roar,
he had to see what was happening.

A pack of wild dragons surrounded
Bing, Bam, and Boom!
"We're not going to let any wild
dragons bully our boys, are we?"
Stoick yelled.

Thornado and the other dragons
raced back to Dragon Island.
Then Thornado used his roar
to scare the wild dragons away.
Toothless and Meatlug helped too!

At last the baby Thunderdrums
were safe!
But what if the wild dragons
came back?
Bing, Bam, and Boom were too young
to be alone.
Stoick knew what he had to do.

Stoick removed Thornado's saddle.
"Take care of your new family,"
he said. "Good-bye, old friend."
It wasn't easy to say good-bye,
but Stoick knew it was right.
Thornado was a great dragon,
and now he would be a great dad!